Teggs is no ordinary dinosaur –
he's an **ASTROSAUR!** Captain of
the amazing spaceship DSS *Sauropod*,
he goes on dangerous missions and
fights evil – along with his faithful
crew, Gipsy, Arx and Iggy!

Collect all the **Astrosaurs!**
Free collector cards in every book
for you to swap with your friends.
More cards available from the
Astrosaurs website –
www.astrosaurs.co.uk

Astrosaurs

THE SEAS
OF DOOM

Steve Cole

Illustrated by
Woody Fox

RED FOX

THE SEAS OF DOOM
A RED FOX BOOK 9780099472964

First published in Great Britain in 2005 by Red Fox,
an imprint of Random House Children's Books

5 7 9 10 8 6

The Random House Group Limited makes every effort to ensure that the
papers used in its books are made from trees that have been legally sourced
from well-managed and credibly certified forests. Our paper procurement
policy can be found at: www.randomhouse.co.uk/paper.htm

Set in Bembo Schoolbook

Red Fox books are published by Random House Children's Books
61-63 Uxbridge Road, London W5 5SA,
a division of the Random House Group Ltd

Addresses for companies within The Random House Group Limited can be
found at: www.randomhouse.co.uk/offices.htm

THE RANDOM HOUSE GROUP Limited Reg. No. 954009
www.kidsatrandomhouse.co.uk

A CIP catalogue record for this book is available from the British Library

Printed in the UK by CPI Bookmarque Ltd, Croydon, CR0 4TD

For Annie and James

WARNING!

THINK YOU KNOW ABOUT DINOSAURS?

THINK AGAIN!

The dinosaurs . . .

Big, stupid, lumbering reptiles. Right?

All they did was eat, sleep and roar a bit. Right?

Died out millions of years ago when a big meteor struck the Earth. Right?

Wrong!

The dinosaurs weren't stupid. They may have had small brains, but they used them well. They had big thoughts and big dreams.

By the time the meteor hit, the last dinosaurs had already left Earth for ever. Some breeds had discovered how to travel through space as early as the Triassic period, and were already enjoying a new life among the stars. No one has found evidence of dinosaur technology yet. But the first fossil bones were only unearthed in 1822, and new finds are being made all the time.

The proof is out there, buried in the ground.

And the dinosaurs live on, way out in space, even now. They've settled down in a place they call the Jurassic Quadrant and over the last sixty-five million years they've gone on evolving.

The dinosaurs we'll be meeting are

part of a special group called the Dinosaur Space Service. Their job is to explore space, to go on exciting missions and to fight evil and protect the innocent!

These heroic herbivores are not just dinosaurs.

They are *astrosaurs!*

NOTE: The following story has been translated from secret Dinosaur Space Service records. Earthling dinosaur names are used throughout, although some changes have been made for easy reading. There's even a guide to help you pronounce the dinosaur names at the back of the book.

THE CREW OF THE DSS SAUROPOD

CAPTAIN TEGGS STEGOSAUR

ARX ORANO, FIRST OFFICER

GIPSY SAURINE, COMMUNICATIONS OFFICER

IGGY TOOTH, CHIEF ENGINEER

Jürassic Quadrant

Ankylos

Steggos

Diplox

INDEPENDEN
DINOSAUR
ALLIANCE

vegetarian
sector

Squawk
Major

DSS
UNION OF
PLANETS

PTEROSAURIA

Tri System

Corytho

Lambeos

Iguanos

Aqua Minor

OUTER SPACE

Geldos Cluster

Teerex Major

Olympus

TYRANNOSAUR
TERRITORIES

Planet Sixty

carnivore
sector

Raptos

THEROPOD EMPIRE

Megalos

Cryptos

vegmeat
zone
(neutral space)

SEA REPTILE
SPACE

Pliosaur
Nurseries

Not to scale

THE SEAS
OF DOOM

Chapter One

A SOGGY MISSION

In orbit high above the planet Aqua
Minor, Captain Teggs Stegosaur was
waiting to start his next adventure.

He was waiting *very* impatiently.

"Admiral Rosso had better call us
soon," Teggs grumbled, chomping on the
delicious moss that
covered his control
pit. "I can't wait to
find out why
we've been sent to
the soggiest
planet in the
Jurassic
Quadrant!"

"I'm sure it won't be much longer, Captain," said Arx Orano, the triceratops beside him.

Sitting around twiddling his thumbs wasn't easy for the young, daredevil stegosaurus. He didn't have any thumbs, for a start.

Teggs commanded the DSS *Sauropod*, the finest ship in the Dinosaur Space Service. He and his crew were all highly trained astrosaurs. They flew through space helping plant-eaters in peril – wherever the planet, whatever the risk.

But why had the *Sauropod* been sent to a world full of *fish*?

"Maybe Admiral Rosso thinks we need a holiday by the seaside," said Iggy Tooth, the *Sauropod*'s Chief Engineer. A brave iguanodon, he was clever with machines and fiercely loyal to his captain. "I don't really like the seaside. I'm not keen on fish. I met a fish with no eyes, once."

"That would make it a *fsh*. Get it?" called Gipsy Saurine from her seat. Gipsy was a duck-billed hadrosaur with scaly, stripy skin. She handled the ship's communications and much more besides. "Anyway, there *is* no seaside on Aqua Minor. Only sea!"

"Calling Captain Teggs . . ." The gruff voice of Admiral Rosso, the crusty old barosaurus in charge of the Dinosaur Space Service, suddenly crackled from the *Sauropod*'s speakers. "Captain Teggs, can you hear me?"

"At last!" spluttered Teggs through a mouthful of moss. He rose up from the control pit – eight metres long from tail to beak, with jagged bony plates running down his orange-brown back.

Gipsy trotted over to Teggs. "Shall I put the admiral on the scanner screen, Captain?" she asked.

"Yes please," said Teggs.

Gipsy whistled the order through her snout to the dimorphodon. These plucky pterosaurs were the *Sauropod*'s flight crew, and they loved to be bossed about.

The team leader flapped down and pecked the scanner control happily

with his beak. A moment later, Admiral
Rosso's wrinkled face appeared.

"Ah, there you are, Teggs," said the
old barosaurus. "Sorry to keep you
waiting, but running an entire space
fleet keeps me busy. And when you get
to my age . . ."

Teggs saluted. "What's up, sir?"

"It's what's *down* that's worrying us,"
said Admiral Rosso. "Down below!"

Arx and Gipsy swapped puzzled looks.
But Teggs just smiled at the thought of
a brand new adventure beginning at
last.

"Something very big and very dangerous is swimming about in the seas of Aqua Minor," the admiral went on. "The cryptoclidus who go fishing there are getting very worried."

Teggs frowned. "Crypto-who?"

"A race of sea reptiles from the planet Cryptos," Arx explained. "They have run out of food in their own world, so now they fish the waters of Aqua Minor for squid and shellfish. Then they send it by rocket to the folk back home."

"Very good, Arx," smiled Admiral Rosso. "Teggs, you have a first-rate first officer there!"

"He's the best," Teggs agreed. "So, what's been happening on Aqua Minor?"

"Five undersea fish factories have been

wrecked, along with several submarines."
Admiral Rosso sighed. "But no one
knows who's doing it – or why!"

Teggs nodded. "And you want us to
find out."

"That's right," said Admiral Rosso.
"The cryptoclidus may not be
vegetarians, but they are still our
friends and neighbours in
space. They've asked us for
help in solving this mystery."

"So what are we waiting
for?" asked Teggs. "Let's get
to Aqua Minor and see
what we can find!"

Once Admiral Rosso had given them a
map and some orders, Teggs, Gipsy and
Arx went to the shuttle bay. The air was
smoky and thick with the smell of the
burning dung that fuelled the engines.
Iggy Tooth was waiting for them by the
shuttle.

"The engines are all fired up, Captain!" said the stocky iguanodon. "We're ready to go!"

Once they were safely strapped in, the shuttle blasted off. Soon they were soaring through the brilliant blue skies of Aqua Minor.

"Wow!" said Teggs, peering through the window. "What a view. There's so much sea to see!"

Below them, the ocean stretched out endlessly to the horizon. Enormous spaceships floated above the waves, trailing fishing nets behind them. Teggs watched one spaceship rise higher than the rest. Its net was bulging with shimmering, silvery shellfish that sparkled in the bright sunlight.

"No wonder the cryptoclidus need our help," said Arx. "This is a very big ocean for something nasty to hide in."

"Where are we going to park the shuttle?" asked Iggy.

"On one of their floating factories," said Gipsy, checking her wrist tracker. "It's not far from here."

"It was the first place to be attacked, a month ago," said Teggs. "We'll take a look and search for clues."

Soon the floating factory came into sight. It looked like a large square of shiny metal, covered in long huts. In the middle of the square, a small, grey shape started waving at them.

"Who's that?" asked Iggy, as they came in to land.

"That must be Commander Cripes," said Arx. "He'll be showing us around."

The shuttle landed safely, and its doors slid open. A strong smell of shellfish filled the air.

As the astrosaurs stepped outside, Cripes came waddling up to greet them. Like all cryptoclidus, he looked like a cross between a seal and the Loch Ness monster. He had a long neck and four flat flippers, and his belly dragged on the ground as he moved. A broad-brimmed hat was perched on his head, and a shiny cape kept the sun off his long, smooth back.

"Welcome to Aqua Minor, guys," said Cripes. "Admiral Rosso said you were on your way. Glad you could make it!"

"Thanks," said Teggs. "This is Arx, and this is Iggy."

Cripes smiled. "And this cute little hadrosaur just *has* to be Gipsy." He took her hoof in his flipper and kissed it. "Now, let me show you around. This factory stretches down almost to the sea bed . . ."

Cripes led them into a hut and then into a large lift. It took them down deep under the water. When it finally stopped, Teggs led the way out into a large, crumbling workplace. The machines and conveyor belts stood silent. The walls were cracked. The floor was flooded with smelly, oily water.

"Hard to believe that this place was brand new six weeks ago, isn't it?" sighed Cripes. "Just two weeks after opening, *this* happened."

Teggs stared around. "Something has torn the whole place apart!"

"And this was just the first attack,"

Cripes reminded him. "In the last month there have been lots more. Every new factory we build in this area gets wrecked!"

"What are they used for anyway?" asked Gipsy.

"The floating factories prepare the fish we catch before we send it back home to feed our people," Cripes explained.

"On the bottom

levels, we suck in thousands of ammonites and belemnites from the pens on the sea bed. We take off the shells and rinse them clean. And then a submarine delivers them here for packaging."

"We're under the sea, aren't we?" asked Iggy. "So how come this place isn't full of water?"

"We cryptoclidus live on land as well as in the sea," Cripes reminded him.

16

"The food is easier to pack when it's not floating around all over the place!"

Arx plodded over to a wall and prodded a button with his longest horn. Everyone jumped as the machines sparked into life. The conveyor belt jerked forwards. Metal scoops swung down from the wonky ceiling.

"Cool — the machines still work!" shouted Teggs over all the noise. "What do they do?"

"The shellfish plop out of this pipe here onto the conveyor belt," Cripes explained over the din. "Then they're wrapped up in the wrapping machine and sent upstairs to the spaceships. But nothing has come through that pipe for weeks and in the meantime, the people back home are going hungry."

Teggs felt sad watching the ruined machines clanking away with no purpose. But before he could turn them off, he felt the ground shake beneath his feet.

"That's not the builders starting work on the repairs already, is it?" asked Gipsy nervously.

Suddenly, the whole factory rocked as if a giant had kicked it. The astrosaurs were knocked off their feet. The cracks in the walls widened. The floor broke open beneath them, and sea water began rushing in.

"Never mind the builders!" cried Teggs over the din of the machines and the churning water. "I think the thing that attacked this place before has come back to finish it off!"

Chapter Two

THE SINISTER SHADOW

"Quick, you guys!" yelled Commander Cripes. "Back to the lift!"

Iggy and Gipsy didn't need telling twice. They quickly splashed over to the lift. Teggs and Arx began to follow. But before they could reach the others, the floor before them crumbled away into the water.

"We're cut off!" cried Arx.

"Iggy! Gipsy!" shouted Teggs. "Get out of here now, while you can!"

"But we can't leave you!" called Gipsy. "You'll drown!"

"That's an order!" Teggs bellowed.

Iggy sadly saluted him, and Cripes

pressed a button. The lift clanked slowly upwards.

"We'll get help!" Gipsy called. Then they were gone.

Arx yelped as a large chunk of falling ceiling nearly squashed him. "Come away from the edge, Captain!" he shouted. "If you fall down there you'll never get out again!"

"Wait!" Teggs called, rooted to the spot. "Look! Something's moving down there!"

Arx edged closer. Sure enough he saw a dark shadow in the oily water. It looked like the shadow of something very big and very, very dangerous.

"If only we could get a closer look at it," said Teggs.

"Captain," Arx gasped. "If the water level keeps rising, *it* might swim up here to get a closer look at *us*!"

Together they backed away from the edge. The freezing cold water was now up to their chins.

"This looks like the end," sighed Arx.

"We'll find a way out," said Teggs bravely. He tried to think, but it wasn't easy with the noise of the clanking machines all around him.

Then he had a brainwave.

"The machines!" he cried. "If we can climb up onto the machines, we'll be higher up. The water will take longer to reach us!"

Teggs grabbed hold of one of the dangling scoops with his beak. He used it to haul himself up onto the clanking conveyor belt. Arx tried to do the same, but he struggled. Teggs wrapped his tail round the triceratops's head frill and helped him up.

"Now the water only comes up to our toes!" beamed Teggs.

"But we're heading for the wrapping machine!" cried Arx. "It'll squash us into a parcel!"

"No, it won't," said Teggs, smashing his big, bony tail into the machine. It exploded in a cloud of sparks. "I think it's out of order!" he grinned.

As the sparks died away, the machines suddenly stopped. The room fell eerily quiet. The only sound was the swoosh of the sea water beneath them.

"I guess I caused a short circuit," said Teggs.

"At least we can hear ourselves think now," said Arx. He paused. "Er, Captain . . . can you hear what I hear?"

Teggs listened. "I can't hear anything."

"Exactly!" said Arx. "Whatever was attacking us, it seems to have given up!"

Teggs peered over the edge of the conveyor belt. There was no sign of the dark shadow beneath the sea. "I think you're right," he whispered.

But then something large and white came whizzing up through the water.

"Look out!" yelled Teggs.

The big white thing burst out of the sea below them with a massive splash. A huge wave of water crashed over Teggs and Arx, blinding them both.

"It's a sea monster!" shouted Arx, blinking furiously.

"Get behind me, Arx!" cried Teggs, his eyes stinging. "I'll fight it off!"

"Actually," said a familiar voice, "I only wanted to give you a lift!"

Teggs grinned with delight as he blinked away the last of the saltwater. "Iggy!" he cheered.

The big white thing was only the shuttle. Now it bobbed about on the water in front of them, like a giant rubber duck in a very big bath. Iggy stood in the doorway.

Gipsy leaned out behind him and waved. "We thought this might be a good time to see if the shuttle works underwater."

"Luckily it does!" added Cripes, peering over Gipsy's shoulder. "At least for short trips!"

"Good work, guys," said Teggs as he leaped aboard. "Come on, there's no time to lose. We just saw something very big swimming about down here. Let's try to follow it!"

"That's risky, Captain," said Arx. "That thing must be big enough to swallow the shuttle in one gulp!"

"It's a risk we'll have to take," Teggs told him.

Once Arx had scrambled into the shuttle, they set off. Like a submarine, the little ship ducked under the waves and hummed quietly through the clear green water. But all they saw were shoals of tiny fish swimming past them. There was no sign of the mysterious dark thing.

"How could it just vanish?" wondered Teggs.

Suddenly a warning light came on in the shuttle.

"Sea water is getting into the engine pipes," said Iggy.

"OK, Iggy," sighed Teggs. "Better head back to the surface, fast!"

"Aye-aye, Captain," said Iggy.

He steered the shuttle sharply upwards. A few seconds later, it burst from the sea like a great white whale. The warning light went out, and everyone breathed a sigh of relief.

Teggs turned to Cripes. "Is there somewhere we can go to plan our next move?"

"The nearest base is Sea Station One, fifty miles north of here. It's where the fishing teams live while they're staying on Aqua Minor."

"Will the shuttle get us that far?" asked Arx.

"Just about," said Iggy. "We don't have enough power to fly, but we can chug along the surface like a motorboat!"

"Good," said Teggs with a grin. "I just hope there'll be some food about. I'm *starving!*"

Chapter Three

DEEP DOWN DANGER

"Wow!" said Gipsy as the shuttle sailed into sight of Sea Station One. It was like a cross between a grand hotel, a beautiful harbour and a busy spaceport. Some cryptoclidus were splashing about in enormous pools of salty water. Others sat in cafés eating buckets of fish.

In the distance, rockets blasted off from the floating factories, filled with food to take home to Cryptos. And as Gipsy followed her friends off the shuttle, a large oily tugboat sailed in to the sea station, filled with gangs of chattering cryptoclidus.

She turned to Cripes. "What do you need old-fashioned boats for? I thought you had spaceships to pull your nets?"

"The tugboats ferry our workers to and from the floating factories," Cripes explained. "Few of us dare to swim in the sea at the moment."

"Well, we'll have to *sea* what we can do about that," Teggs chuckled.

"Have you marked where the monster attacks took place?" asked Arx.

Cripes took out a map of Aqua
Minor from his raincoat and Gipsy
helped him unfold it. "X marks the
spot," he said. "*Several* spots."

"So all five attacks took place in the
south of the planet," noted Arx.

"That's right," said Cripes. "All our
other floating factories are in the north.
We've been trying to build new ones in
the south to meet the demand for
shellfish back home . . ."

"But every single one has been
destroyed," growled Iggy.

"It looks like someone – or something – is fed up with you fishing here," said Gipsy.

"And it's our job to find out who," said Teggs bravely. "Once we've had a quick snack . . ."

"Of course." Cripes led them to the nearest café and slapped his flippers together. A waiter paddled straight over with a massive plate of sticky, slimy seaweed. Teggs took a cautious nibble. It tasted like a wet, salty dishcloth.

"Delicious," gasped Teggs weakly. "But perhaps I'll skip the snack. I should start searching the sea."

"I'll come with you," said Gipsy.

"You know it's risky," Cripes warned them.

"Of course," beamed Teggs. "But if we're to help you, we need to find out more."

33

"I wish I could let you guys take a sub," said Cripes. "But we don't have any left. We tried looking for the monster in them. But the subs are so noisy, I guess the monster heard us coming a mile away. It chewed them all up!"

Gipsy looked worried. "Did the pilots get out?"

"Only just," said Cripes. "They were lucky to escape with their lives! But by the time they'd wriggled out of the wrecks, there was no sign of the monster at all." He clicked his tongue. "Oh, well. Maybe you'll have more luck in the diving bell."

"What's a diving bell?" asked Teggs.

"It's like a big metal case with a window in the side," Arx explained. "It'll take you underwater!"

"We take you out to sea," said Cripes. "Then we lower you down into the water on a chain so you can take a good look about."

"How will we breathe?" asked Teggs.

"It's completely airtight," Cripes assured him. "But there's also deep-sea diving gear on board in case of emergencies."

"What if we get into trouble?" asked Gipsy.

"Just press the help button," said Cripes. "We'll have you back out again in no time!"

"Fair enough," said Teggs. "Meanwhile, I'd like Arx to check over those chewed-up subs for clues."

"No problem," Cripes told him. "They're all piled up in a storeroom downstairs."

"Can I see some wreckage from that floating factory, too?" asked Arx.

"We'll pick some up for you." Cripes

rose and adjusted his hat. "Well, if you guys are ready . . ."

"We sure are!" Teggs jumped to his feet. "Let's get going!"

The shuttle's engines were still soggy, so Cripes took them out in one of the tugboats to the wreck of the floating factory. Teggs was wearing his battle armour, and Gipsy had slipped on her combat suit.

"I've never tried using my electro-tail underwater," said Teggs thoughtfully.

"Arx said our armour would work wherever we were," said Gipsy. "And if we do meet any monsters down there, I'm glad about that!"

Once they had reached the wreck, Teggs and Gipsy squeezed inside the orange diving bell.

There was just room for the two of them and the diving gear.

Cripes waved at them through the window. "On top of the bell is a special camera," he said. "It can see through murky water. So if you *do* find a nasty sea monster down there, we should get a good picture of it."

"We'll ask it to say cheese," joked Teggs.

"Good luck, guys," said Cripes. Iggy pressed a big green button, and Gipsy squealed as the bell was heaved up over the side of the ship on heavy chains.

"This is better than a funfair ride!" Teggs declared. He looked out through the large window in the side of the bell. On the ship's deck, Iggy stood beside Cripes. He gave a small, worried wave to his captain.

Slowly, the diving bell was lowered into the water. Teggs and Gipsy were soon staring out at an undersea world. Curious fish swam up to see them.

Deeper and deeper they went. A friendly squid blinked at them as it drifted by. A weird, spindly fish spiralled lazily past.

The bell came to rest on the sea bed with a soft bump. The water through the window was cloudy and dark. Nothing moved. Nothing stirred at all.

Gipsy felt a shiver go through her. "I hope this thing doesn't leak," she said.

Teggs nodded. "Let's put on the diving gear, just in case."

They helped each other strap oxygen tanks to their necks. Then they put on special diving helmets.

"Now we'll be ready for anything," beamed Teggs.

But neither of them was ready for what happened next.

Wham!

The diving bell shook with an enormous blow.

"What was that?" gasped Gipsy.

"I don't know!" said Teggs. He peered out of the window — and wished he hadn't.

A massive sea monster was staring in at them with huge, yellow eyes. Its skin was a deep blotchy blue and white. Its head was the size of a sofa, and the top of it was wrapped in a tatty bandage. It was easily three times as long as Teggs, and its flippers were the size of small trees.

The sea monster smiled, revealing a long row of terrifying teeth. Then it attacked the diving bell. Its teeth tore through the metal like it was wet cardboard. Sea water flooded in through the gaping hole in the wall.

"Hit the help button, Gipsy!" cried Teggs. "It's coming to get us!"

Chapter Four

THE MONSTER

Up on the tugboat, the chain holding the diving bell was swinging about like a piece of string in a gale.

"Something's wrong!" gasped Iggy. "Quick! Bring up the bell!"

Cripes hit a yellow button on his control panel. The chain clanked and heaved – but the diving bell wouldn't rise.

"It's jammed!" cried Cripes. "Something's got hold of it!"

"I'll boost the power," said Iggy. He fiddled with some wires beneath the control panel. "Try it now!"

Cripes pressed the button again. This time, the bell began to move from the sea bed.

He beamed at Iggy. "You did it!"

Iggy and Cripes waited tensely. Finally, the diving bell emerged from the foaming waters.

Or what was left of it.

The bell had been mangled and squashed. Half of it was missing altogether. But most worrying of all, it was completely empty.

"Teggs and Gipsy . . ." breathed Iggy. "They've gone!"

"But so has their diving gear," said Cripes, peering inside. "Maybe they got away."

"If they did, they're still too heavy to swim up from the bottom of the sea!" wailed Iggy. "We have to find them – fast!"

Cripes clapped his flippers. Two

cryptoclidus sailors in white caps and overalls slithered up to him.

"We need to get a search party down there, guys," said Cripes. "Ten of your fastest swimmers, right now!"

The two sailors nodded. "Straight away, sir," they cried, and then dashed off.

Iggy sighed, wishing the shuttle worked better underwater so he could look for himself. "How long can Teggs and Gipsy stay down there?"

"Let me see . . ." Cripes counted on his flippers. "They should have enough air to last three hours. After that . . ."

Iggy looked very glum. "I suppose I'd better tell Arx the bad news," he said.

"We won't just tell him," said Cripes gravely. "We'll *show* him." He pointed a flipper at the mangled diving bell. "The undersea camera is still there. We'll take it back with us and see just what happened."

"Well, what are we waiting for?" cried Iggy. "Let's get going!"

★

45

Iggy and Cripes found Arx busy
working in the storeroom full of broken
subs and wreckage from the floating
factory. When the triceratops heard
what had happened to the diving bell,
his horns seemed to droop.

"Don't worry, Arx. The search party
will find them soon and carry them
safely back up to the surface," said Iggy
stoutly. "Right, Cripes?"

"I hope so," said Cripes. He pulled out
the camera from under his cape. "In the

meantime, these pictures should be ready. Let's see what happened down there."

Arx and Iggy gathered round him as he pulled the back off the camera. Inside was a set of pictures, bone-dry and crystal-clear. Always impressed by a good invention, Arx was about to compliment Cripes on his clever camera. But he lost his voice when he saw what the pictures showed.

One showed the massive blue and white monster swimming up to the bell.

Another showed its enormous flippers and terrible tail.

"Look at the size of that thing!" gasped Cripes. "It's as big as a battleship!"

He quickly
sorted through
more of the
pictures. They
showed the
monster grinning wildly, and then
tearing through the metal of the diving
bell. It seemed dead set on getting to
Gipsy and Teggs.

"It should pick on someone its own
size," said Iggy fiercely.

Cripes gulped. "There *is* no one else
its own size!"

 The second-to-
last picture showed
Teggs and Gipsy
standing on the sea
bed in their diving
gear. They were
looking up at the fearsome creature.

"No!" groaned Iggy. "I don't want to
see what happened next!"

"I'm afraid we must," said Arx quietly.

But the last of
the pictures
showed only the
empty sea bed.

"Where did
they go?" demanded Iggy. "It's like they
just vanished!"

"At least there's no sign that they
were hurt," said Cripes.

Arx nodded slowly. "And at least now
we know that a *liopleurodon* is hiding
down there in the deeps," he said.

Iggy frowned. "A what?"

"Back on Earth it was the biggest,
nastiest killing machine in the water!"
Arx went on. "You're looking at one
hundred tons of swimming death!"

"It . . . it can't be true!" stammered
Cripes. "The liopleurodon rule those
huge water worlds on the edge of the
Jurassic Quadrant. No one has visited
them for hundreds of years – they
wouldn't dare!"

"Maybe not," said Arx darkly. "But it seems the liopleurodon have dared to visit Aqua Minor!"

"If it *is* just a visit," growled Iggy. "This could be the start of an invasion!"

"But I don't understand!" Cripes started shivering. "A liopleurodon ship couldn't land here without us knowing about it. And we've been fishing on Aqua Minor for five years without any trouble!"

"Oh, come on! Wakey-wakey!" cried Iggy. He waved the pictures in Cripes's face. "What more proof do you need? There's a liopleurodon out there! It's

 been smashing up your factories, eating your subs and scaring everyone silly – and now it's got Teggs and Gipsy!"

Chapter Five

A STRANGE FRIEND

Back at the bottom of the sea, Teggs and Gipsy were facing up to the massive monster with the bandaged head.

Once the liopleurodon had ripped apart the diving bell, he floated in the water, watching them closely. Teggs had pulled his scariest face and swished his armoured tail through the water. Gipsy was ready to jab their attacker on the nose if he came any closer.

But they were both surprised to find that the liopleurodon had no plans to eat them alive.

In fact, he was very polite.

"Right then!" he said brightly. Bubbles streamed out of his mouth as he spoke. "I've got you out of that horrible prison. Now you can come home with me!"

Teggs and Gipsy stared at each other in amazement

through their diving helmets.

"What do you mean?" Gipsy cried. "That wasn't a prison!"

"Of course it was!" said the liopleurodon. "You were both squished up inside! Trapped by those flipper-flappers! Locked up and hanging from a chain! But now you're free!"

The sea monster smiled happily. He was clearly very pleased with himself.

Teggs turned to Gipsy. "What's a flipper-flapper?"

"It must be his word for the cryptoclidus," Gipsy whispered back.

Teggs cleared his throat. "Well, thanks for trying to help," he said. "But without that, er, *prison* as you call it, we can't get back up to the surface!"

"Why would you want to do that?" asked the liopleurodon, baffled. "The flipper-flappers would only lock you up again. No, no, the likes of us should stick together."

"What do you mean?" asked Gipsy.

"Well, *you're* not flipper-flappers. *I'm* not a flipper-flapper. But everyone else on the planet *is*!"

Teggs looked at him thoughtfully. "Who are you?"

"I think my name must be Mira," said the liopleurodon. "That's what is written

on my outfit,
anyway!" He
spun round to
show them a
torn scrap of
blue uniform
that clung to
his middle. The
word MIRA was
spelled out in gold thread.

"You mean you don't even know your
own *name*?" asked Teggs.

"Nope!" said Mira cheerfully. "I must
have been bumped on the head at some
point. I'm sure I'm not just wearing this
bandage because it looks pretty."

"That's for sure," murmured Gipsy.

"Anyway," said Mira. "Now that I've
set you free, you must help me find my
spaceship! I'm sure I parked it round
here somewhere, but that was a long,
long time ago." He gave a sad little
sigh. "I've been searching ever since."

"You parked a spaceship under the sea?" Teggs turned to Gipsy. "Bump on the head or not, this so-called sea monster is a nut!" he hissed.

Gipsy nodded. "But he's a very big, very dangerous nut with *extremely* big teeth!" she pointed out. "We'd better not upset him."

"Well?" asked Mira. His gleaming eyes narrowed a little. "*Are* you going to help me?"

Teggs gulped. "Umm . . . Yes."

"Hurrah!" cried Mira, brightening again. "I know it's round here somewhere. We're bound to find it soon. Follow me!"

Gipsy cleared her throat. "Actually, I think we should stay here—"

"Follow me!" Mira yelled crossly, cutting her off. "My cave is this way."

Teggs and Gipsy couldn't move very fast underwater. They shivered in the awful cold. Their heavy bodies ached as they trudged over the thick dark sand.

"We have to get back to the surface," muttered Gipsy. "We don't have enough air to stay down here for long."

"I know," said Teggs. "But how?"

Mira kept swimming round them in a big circle. "Keep up!" he yelled. "I can't wait to show you my cave! It's ever so cosy, and you'll love the colours! I've chosen brown rock, with bits of darker brown rock and just a hint of very, *very* brown rock . . ."

"This Mira is as batty as a belemnite," said Teggs quietly. "But he seems friendly enough."

Gipsy nodded. "So why has he been attacking factories and submarines?"

"What?" asked Mira, zooming up behind them. "Me? Attack factories and submarines? Why would I do that?"

"You tell us," said Teggs bravely. "That's what you've been doing, isn't it?"

"Don't be so silly," said Mira, floating upside down and going cross-eyed. "I've never attacked a factory in my life! I stay well away from those flipper-flappers with their big nets. I don't want to get caught!"

Gipsy turned back to Teggs. "Do you believe him?" she whispered.

"I don't know," said Teggs. "But why would he bother to lie? He could eat us alive in a couple of bites!"

"Stop chatting and get a move on!" nagged Mira. "Honestly, dinner will be ruined!"

Teggs perked up. "Dinner?"

"Yes!" cried Mira, waggling his flippers. "Din-dins! Come on! Come and get it!"

"Brilliant!" Teggs quickened his step. He was still starving.

"But *Captain* . . ." Gipsy tapped his diving helmet with her hoof. "How are you going to eat through *that* thing?"

"Arrgh!" Teggs groaned. "I'm going as nutty as Mira!"

But when they finally reached the liopleurodon's lair, Teggs found he was glad to miss Mira's meal. It was floating all about them in the cold, dark water — tons and tons of raw, rotten squid!

"Come on, chaps! Dig in!" Mira beamed. "Took me ages to catch this lot!"

"Oh." Gipsy swapped an awkward look with Teggs. "Sorry, Mira, but we're, er, not really hungry."

"Not hungry?" Mira looked hurt. "But . . . I wanted to celebrate meeting you. I've been very lonely down here on my own, you know." Mira opened his giant jaws and guzzled down fifty squid in a single gulp. "So take those glass hats off your heads and tuck in!"

"We can't!" said Teggs.

"Of course you can," said Mira briskly. "No need to be shy."

"But we can't breathe in water like you do," Teggs protested.

Mira folded his fins firmly. "Take them *off*."

"If we do, we'll drown!" cried Gipsy.

"Drown? Don't be so silly!" said Mira crossly. "Only the flipper-flappers

breathe air. *We* live in the sea!" He
came closer. "And if you won't take off
those silly glass bubbles yourselves . . .
I'll take them off for you!"

Mira's mouth swung open, revealing
rows of lethal teeth, as he lunged
towards them . . .

Chapter Six

HIDE AND SEEK

Teggs and Gipsy dived out of the way –
just in time. Mira's razor-sharp teeth
scratched the side of Gipsy's glass helmet.
"Let me wear it, *please!*" she begged Mira.
"What a lot of fuss you're making!"
Mira tutted. "The silly
thing doesn't
even suit you!"
He opened
his mouth
again to pluck
off Gipsy's
diving helmet.
This time, he
couldn't miss . . .

Teggs flexed his armoured tail, ready to whack Mira right on the flipper. But as his tail swung back it struck some rotten squid floating in the water. The power in his armour sparked through them – and made them glow a spooky electric blue!

Mira moaned in horror. "Ghosts!" he cried. "My breakfast has come back to haunt me!" A cloud of bubbles burst from his behind. "Aaaaagh!"

With that, the terrified giant sped from the cave.

"What a brilliant plan, Captain!" said Gipsy admiringly. "But how did you know that using your electro-tail underwater would light up anything it touched?"

Teggs stared at the glowing squid. He was almost as surprised as Mira. Then he grinned. "You know me, Gipsy," he said. "I may have a brain the size of an acorn, but I've always been a bright spark! Come on, let's get out of here before Mira comes back!"

They quickly left the cave. The water was dark and gloomy as they tried to retrace their steps across the sea bed. But it was hard to tell which way they should go. At the bottom of the sea, everything looked the same – dark and spooky.

Soon, Teggs and Gipsy realized they were totally lost.

"We're running out of air, Captain," said Gipsy.

"Someone will find us soon!" Teggs said confidently.

"Yoo-hoo!" came Mira's voice.

"Oh no," groaned Teggs. "I didn't mean *him*!"

"Hello?" The liopleurodon was getting closer. "Where are you?"

The two astrosaurs ducked down behind some clumps of seaweed.

"The ghosts have gone!" he shouted. "You can come back now!" Then his mouth opened in a big smile. "Oh, I see! It's a game! Hide and seek! Can't we play hunt the spaceship instead? I know it's round here somewhere . . ."

Mira swam closer, his massive head searching this way and that. Soon he would find them.

"Run for it!" hissed Teggs.

Together, the two astrosaurs sprinted through the murky water. They slipped on slimy seaweed. Coral scraped their legs. Their sides ached with effort.

"Found you!" cried Mira, behind them. "You can't hide from me!"

"We have to keep going," gasped Teggs.

There was a big patch of slimy seaweed ahead. They slipped and skidded over it. Then, with a shout, Teggs fell *through* the seaweed!

Gipsy grabbed hold of his vanishing tail. She tried to pull him back up, but he was too heavy.

With a cry, Gipsy was dragged down through the slimy seaweed after him, into the blackness beyond.

The fall lasted only a few seconds. Teggs went tumbling through the water until he landed on his bottom with a bump. Gipsy landed beside him a second later. They were in a wide tunnel. Although the walls were thick with limpets and seaweed, something shiny was glinting through underneath.

Teggs took a closer look. "This isn't rock. It's metal!" he cried.

"A metal tunnel under the seabed?" Gipsy frowned. "What could it be?"

"Let's find out," he said. The astrosaurs walked cautiously along the tunnel, straining to see through the murky water. Then they came to a doorway. A sign glowed eerily above them:

CONTROL ROOM.

Teggs nodded gravely. "I think we're inside a spaceship!"

"*Mira's* spaceship!" gasped Gipsy. "The one he's trying to find! But what's it doing here?"

"He didn't *park* it under the water," Teggs realized. "He must have *crashed* it into the ocean and right through the sea bed! I think we fell in through a big hole in the roof, hidden by the seaweed."

"But how do we get back out?" wondered Gipsy. "There's no way we can climb out of that hole again! And a search party would never think of looking for us down here. They don't even know this place exists!"

"And on top of all that, our air is running out fast," said Teggs. "Come on, Gipsy. Let's try to find another way back to the sea bed. . ."

Cautiously, they crept on into the gloomy spaceship's control room.

Chapter Seven

A TOOTHY RIDDLE

The sunken spaceship's control room was large and wide with a low ceiling. It was clearly designed for giant sea creatures. The controls were built into the floor, so the crew could work them with their tails and flippers.

Gipsy looked at a plastic newspaper floating in the water "*The Liopleurodon Times*. It's six years old!" she said. "This ship has been down here for six whole years at the very least!"

"So the ship crashed here a year before the cryptoclidus first arrived," Teggs realized. "And the trouble only started when they started building factories around this area."

"Maybe they disturbed something," said Gipsy. "Something dangerous!" Teggs nodded. Then he noticed a metal box on the floor with an aerial on top, half covered by the water. "Hey, Gipsy! This looks familiar . . ."

"It's for sending distress calls!" cried Gipsy. "We've got something like it on the *Sauropod*." She looked closely at the box. "It's broken. But maybe I can fix it!"

"Try!" Teggs urged her. "If we could only send an SOS to Sea Station One . . ."

He waited anxiously while Gipsy went to work with her delicate claws. Finally she gave a small hoot of success. "I think I've got it working," she said. "But there's not much power. The signal is very weak."

"Someone will hear it," said Teggs quietly. "They *must*."

With nothing to do but wait, the astrosaurs moved on into the cold shadows of the creepy ship.

Meanwhile, back on Sea Station One, Iggy and Arx were hard at work down in the storeroom. The two of them had been waiting ages for news of Teggs and Gipsy. They were worried sick.

Arx was still checking over the chewed-up wreckage. He was patiently comparing sections of sub, fragments of floating factory and bits of the diving bell.

Iggy had talked some cryptoclidus sailors into helping him fix one of the broken subs. They were busy in the room next door, hammering out dents in the sub's metal body and fixing all the instruments. Iggy himself had taken tiny pieces from all the subs and was using them to build a brand new engine. Now it was ready for testing, so he switched it on.

With a gentle hum, the engine started up first time.

"I've done it!" cried Iggy. "This new engine is ten times better and fifty times quieter than the old ones!"

Then the door to the storeroom flew open as Cripes splashed inside.

Arx and Iggy spoke together. "Well?"

"The search party can't find a thing down there," said Cripes. "But every radio in the place is picking up some kind of weird SOS call! It seems to be coming from somewhere *beneath* the sea bed!"

"It *might* be Teggs and Gipsy," cried Arx.

"If they are down there, I'll find them!" vowed Iggy. "My new super-sub is almost ready to go. And it's fitted with all kinds of extra gadgets!"

"But we know that the liopleurodon has a taste for subs," Cripes reminded him. "It chomped all the old ones to pieces!"

Arx cleared his throat. "Actually, that's not true."

Cripes and Iggy stared at him.

"It was not a liopleurodon who chomped up the subs," he went on. "And it was not a liopleurodon who wrecked those floating factories."

"Come on!" Cripes scoffed. "You'll be telling us next that a liopleurodon didn't chew up that diving bell."

"Oh, no," said Arx. "A liopleurodon *definitely* did that." He nodded. "That's how I know it didn't do anything else!"

"How?" asked Cripes.

"Tooth marks!" cried Arx. "Look at that diving bell. It was ripped apart by long, sharp teeth. You can see the marks from here."

"So?" said Iggy.

"So, I haven't found tooth marks like that anywhere else," Arx said.

"Not on *any* of this wreckage."

"What *did* you find?" asked Cripes.

"*Tiny* marks," Arx told him. "Hundreds of thousands of tiny little marks – made by tiny little teeth!"

"But that's impossible," protested Iggy. "You and Captain Teggs both saw a huge shadow in the sea. That has to be the liopleurodon, right?"

"Maybe not," said Arx. "Maybe the liopleurodon is working with something else. Something just as big . . . or maybe even bigger!"

Cripes took off his hat and scratched his head with a flipper. "Strange for something so big to have such teeny-weeny teeth."

"Never mind all that," said Iggy. "Let's get going!" He patted his shiny new engine. "We'll find Captain Teggs and Gipsy. And we'll find whatever else is hiding down there in the deeps, too – whatever it takes!"

Chapter Eight

THE FISH FACTOR

Back beneath the sea bed, Teggs and Gipsy were still exploring the liopleurodon ship. It was cold, dark and scary. And both of them knew that their precious air supply was running out with every breath they took. As they walked along one dark corridor, the dirty water grew chillier. Slowly it was becoming a thick, icy slush.

"Shall we turn back?" asked Gipsy nervously. "We don't want to wind up as dinosaur ice-pops!"

"Just a little further," said Teggs.

The chilly passage ended in what seemed to be a giant freezer. Lying in the middle of the room were four big caskets made of solid ice. Teggs could see the huge dark shape of a liopleurodon lying inside three of them. But the fourth was damaged. Part of the ceiling had collapsed on top of it, and the casket had cracked right open.

"This must be Mira's crew," Gipsy gasped. "Are they dead?"

"Just sleeping, I think," breathed Teggs. "A deep, frozen sleep to keep them fresh while they wait to be rescued. But Mira's woken up ahead of time!"

Gipsy pointed to some blue scraps in the water beside the broken casket. "What are they?"

"Bits of Mira's uniform I think. There's writing on them." Teggs took a closer look. "A and D on this bit. An L on the other. What does that mean?"

"Admiral!" cried Gipsy.

Teggs frowned. "I'm only a captain at the moment!"

"No, I'm talking about Mira!" Gipsy's crest flushed red with excitement, and made her helmet steam up. "He thought his name was Mira because it's written on that scrap of uniform he wears. But that's only *part* of the word. Really it spells AD—MIRA—L!"

"Of course!" breathed Teggs. "Then this really *is* his ship. But the ceiling fell in on his head before he could get into the deep freeze. That must be how he lost his memory!"

"Poor Mira," sighed Gipsy. "He must've slipped out into the sea in a daze, and forgotten how to get back!"

"Yes – and something else may have slipped out with him," said Teggs quietly. "Let's keep looking."

"I wonder how much longer our air will last," said Gipsy quietly. "We can't have much left by now."

"I know," said Teggs. "But we mustn't give up. An astrosaur fights on to the last breath!" He paused. "Sorry, that wasn't a very clever thing to say, was it?"

They left the chilly chamber and took a side-tunnel. Soon they

came to another room. It was marked
LARDER – DO NOT DISTURB. A
huge aquarium stretched along one wall
for hundreds of metres. Nothing moved
in the eerie, dark water.

"This must be where their food lived,"
said Gipsy.

Teggs was puzzled. "Strange to have
an aquarium in a ship that's already full
of water."

"I suppose the fish would swim all
over the ship otherwise, trying to escape
being eaten," Gipsy guessed. Then she
noticed a big hole in the back of the
tank. "Captain! The fish *did* escape!
Look, they must have swum away into
the sea!"

"Good for them," smiled Teggs. "I'm
glad they got out." A thought struck
him. "And if they did, maybe so can
we! If we could find our way back out
to the sea bed, a search party might
spot us!"

"Brilliant!" cried Gipsy.

"All we have to do is break the glass . . ."
He struck the side of the tank with his
tail. The glass glowed a brilliant blue and
a crack appeared in its centre.

But suddenly an alarm went off at ear-
splitting volume. Steel bars slammed
down to block the doorway. They were
trapped inside the larder.

"What did I do?" cried Teggs.

The siren stopped as a helpful computer voice chimed in from a speaker in the ceiling: "You tried to open the fish tank without a password. You are an intruder and a fish-pincher."

Teggs stared up at the speaker. "What would I do with a fish? I'm a vegetarian!"

"A likely story!" snarled the computer. The siren switched on again, only this time it was even louder.

"But there aren't even any fish in the tank!" yelled Teggs.

"Oh yes, there are," said Gipsy. A few deep blue fish had swum inside through the big hole. They came up to the front of the tank, as if to see what was happening. A few others came to join them. Then more. And more. Soon there

were hundreds of fish staring at Gipsy
through the glass.

They didn't seem very happy.

"Turn that siren off!" yelled Teggs. He
tried to bang his tail against the speaker
– but it was just out of reach.

"No way!" snapped the computer.
"I'm going to turn it *up*!" Sure enough,
the siren grew louder still.

"My ears are going to burst!" groaned Teggs. He bashed the steel bars with his tail. They sparked, but held firm. "We can't get out!"

"Never mind *us* getting *out*," said Gipsy fearfully. "Let's just hope those fish can't get *in*!"

"Fish? Why are you bothered about a few fish . . .?"

But Teggs trailed off when he looked at the aquarium.

There were thousands of the tiny creatures now. They had banded together into one enormous group – a huge huddle of angry blue fish, moving and acting as one.

Floating all together, they made Mira seem like a minnow.

"That's the same shape I saw back at the floating factory," Teggs cried over the ear-splitting noise. "It wasn't a giant monster who sank the subs and chewed up the factories after all. It was these

little fish – working together to *act* like
a giant monster!"

Suddenly the dark, seething shape
swept forwards and smashed into the
glass like a living battering ram.

"And now they want to get in here!"
cried Gipsy.

"But why?" wondered Teggs. "What have we done?"

The thousands of fish opened their little mouths and gnashed at the glass. The crack in the side of the tank grew wider.

"Their teeth are as sharp as sharks'!" gasped Gipsy. "I think they're going to eat *us*!"

Chapter Nine

FIN-ISHED?

The great mass of the little blue fish
attacked the side of the tank again. The
crack spread into a pattern of crazy
zigzags, stretching from floor to ceiling.

"Look out, Gipsy!" shouted Teggs.
"They're coming through!"

The fish hurled themselves at the glass, and the tank burst open. Teggs and Gipsy watched helplessly as the tiny creatures swarmed inside the larder . . .

. . . and ignored them completely.

Instead, the fish headed for the speaker in the ceiling, attacking it and tearing it open with their vicious teeth.

The sound of the siren faded.

"Under attack!" gasped the computer voice. "The whisperfish have escaped the larder! Assistance needed—"

Then with a flash of sparks and an electronic cough, the voice and the siren shut off all together.

Teggs' and Gipsy's ears rang in the sudden silence.

And, the next second, the "monster" vanished as all the fish swam swiftly away in different directions. A few of them hung about in the larder, their little mouths opening and closing. But the rest were already swimming back out to sea as if nothing had ever happened.

"Of course!" yelled Teggs at the top of his voice. But some of the fish gave him a nasty look, so he quickly shut up. "They weren't after us. They were after whatever was making the noise!"

"I don't get it," frowned Gipsy.

"You were right," he went on. "The cryptoclidus did disturb something when they built their factories here in the south – those whisperfish! Whisperfish must *hate* noise!"

Gipsy nodded slowly. "Well, the glass in that tank was very thick," she said. "I'll bet it made things ever so quiet in there."

"And once the ship crashed and they escaped, the ocean must have been quiet too," Teggs went on. "Until the cryptoclidus started building in whisperfish waters!"

"Of course!" cried Gipsy. "Ever since then, these whisperfish have been joining together to chew up anything that makes a loud noise – floating factories . . . submarines . . . that silly siren . . . And once they've stopped the racket, they split up again."

"And so the 'monster' seems to vanish!" Teggs nodded. "That's why the whisperfish left us alone in our nice quiet shuttle and the silent diving bell. We weren't disturbing them!"

"Well, now we know what's been going on," said Gipsy. "But what good does it do us? We're almost out of air."

Teggs nodded. He felt a bit dizzy. "If we're not rescued soon . . ."

As he spoke, a massive, dark shape swam up to them through the shattered tank.

"Oh no," groaned Teggs.

It was Mira!

"Coo–eee!" he said, waving a flipper. "I've been looking everywhere for you two! Now, it's my turn to hide . . ." he tailed off. "Wait a moment. This is my spaceship! What are you doing inside my spaceship?"

"Trying to get out!" cried Gipsy.

But then a bright yellow light shone in at them through the glass.

"Don't tell me it's *another* monster!" Teggs groaned.

"It's . . . it's some kind of super submarine!" gasped Gipsy in surprise.

A gleaming sub was gliding through the water towards them.

Mira spun round to see. Then he scowled. "It's those flipper-flappers!" he shouted. "They want to catch us! Well, I'll show them a thing or two!"

With that, he streaked out of the tank and over to the sub. His jaws were open wide.

Teggs stared in horror. "No, Mira, don't!"

But as Mira bit down on the nose of the sub – *Zzzzap!*

His eyes bulged. Then he stuck out his tongue, closed his eyes and fell quietly to the sea bed. A hatch opened on top of the sub and Cripes swam out!

Gipsy hugged Teggs with relief.

"So you *did* hear our SOS signal," smiled Teggs weakly.

Cripes nodded. "Arx worked out the best way to reach you, and Iggy drove us here in record time!" He frowned. "Uh, you're looking kind of . . . blue!"

"We're nearly out of air," gasped Teggs.

"I think I'm going to faint," croaked Gipsy.

"Quick!" cried Cripes. "Into the sub!"

With the last of their strength, Teggs and Gipsy made it aboard. Cripes shut the doors and led them out of the water. Gipsy wriggled out of her helmet and gulped down air. Teggs just swung his head into the wall and broke the glass helmet like an oversized egg.

"That's better!" he whooped. "And have *we* got a story to tell you!"

"Tell me about it when you have had a rest," said Cripes gently. "You two have been through a lot!"

"What happened to Mira?" asked Gipsy.

"He'll be all right," said Cripes. "He's just sleeping. When Iggy fixed up the sub, he also gave it a special force field!"

"Of course," beamed Teggs. "A force field's like a wall of solid energy. When Mira tried to bite it, he got a big shock!"

"Poor Mira," sighed Gipsy. "He's not really bad."

"We'll tow him back to Sea Station One," Teggs declared. "Then we can work out how to get him back home."

The sub's inner door opened and Iggy peered in. "Captain! Gipsy!" he beamed with delight. "You're all right!"

"Just about," sighed Gipsy. She gave Iggy a hug. "Though it's going to take *weeks* to get all the wrinkles out of my skin!"

A few hours later, the astrosaurs were safely back aboard Sea Station One. Teggs and Gipsy were both chilled through from spending so long in the freezing sea. But after a lovely hot bath and a bucket of warm sea-grass, they started to feel a bit better.

The sleeping Mira had been towed to a special undersea pen. The pen was locked, and Cripes had placed guards there. A few hours later, the astrosaurs met Cripes on a balcony above the pen.

"No one is very happy about having a liopleurodon here at Sea Station One," grumbled Cripes.

"If he meant you any harm, don't you think he'd have attacked you already?" said Gipsy.

"I guess so," said Cripes. "Speaking of attacks, thanks for finding the truth behind our mysterious monster! Now all we have to do is catch all the whisperfish and they'll never bother us again!"

Teggs gave Cripes a hard stare. "That doesn't seem fair."

"What do you mean?" asked Cripes.

"It can't be much fun being a

whisperfish on the liopleurodon world,"
said Teggs. "Locked up in a tank and
eaten for lunch – not much of a life, is
it? But here on Aqua Minor, things are
different. The whisperfish have enjoyed a
peaceful life swimming freely in the sea
for years." Teggs marched angrily up to
Cripes. "And what do you want to do
now? You want to catch
them all and send
them back home
for supper!"

"But they're
dangerous!"
Cripes
complained.

"All they
want is some
peace and
quiet," said Arx.
"They've never
bothered you in
the north. They

probably won't bother you in the east and the west, either."

"Share the planet with them, Cripes," Teggs urged him. "Let them live here in peace."

Cripes nodded, a little shamefaced. "You're right. I'm sorry. Of course we'll let them stay!"

"HEY!" came a booming voice from the undersea pen. "What's going on here?"

"It's Mira!" said Teggs. "He's woken up!"

"But he sounds different," said Gipsy. "He sounds really scary!"

Suddenly Mira crashed through the surface of the water and glared up at them. "Who are you?" he bawled. "Who dares to lock *me* up?"

"Don't you recognize us?" said Gipsy.

"Never seen you before!" he shouted. "I'm hungry! What have you done with my whisperfish?"

"They're off the menu," Teggs told him. "Sorry!"

"Sorry? You will be!" snarled the liopleurodon. "I'm Admiral Don Leo of the Liopleurodon Space Fleet! The last thing I remember was crash-landing on this crummy planet during a test flight." His eyes narrowed. "But now I've woken up. And I'm hungry. And I'm very, *very* ANGRY!"

Chapter Ten

ALL WRAPPED UP!

Arx cleared his throat. "It would seem that the liopleurodon's memory has come back," he said. "It must be the shock he got from biting the force field!"

"No one keeps me locked up!" roared Don Leo. "Forget the whisperfish – I'll eat every one of *you* when I get out of here!"

"Oh, dear," sighed Teggs. "We've dealt with one monster. Now here's another one to take its place!"

"There's not a prison built that can hold me!" growled Don Leo. "And I'll prove it!" He swam at top speed towards the side of the pen and bashed it over and over. The wall was thick, but soon cracks were starting to show.

Cripes was trembling. "He's going to get out into the open sea! Think of the damage he could cause!"

"We'll just have to stop him," said Teggs simply. "Cripes, Iggy, let's head for the super-sub – fast!"

With a final roar of rage, Don Leo smashed a huge hole in the side of the pen.

"Now I'm going to eat everyone on this planet!" he yelled.

"Not so fast!" shouted Teggs from the super-sub. "First you'll have to deal with a couple of astrosaurs!"

With that, Iggy turned the super-sub round and revved the dung-powered engines right in Don Leo's furious face.

"That tastes revolting!" Don Leo spluttered. "I'll get you for that!"

The super-sub sped away, the liopleurodon close behind it.

"All right, Cripes," said Teggs. "Where's the nearest floating factory?"

"About three miles north," said Cripes. "But it's a brand new building. We've only just put all the machines in."

"Perfect!" cried Teggs. "Well away from the whisperfish. Iggy, get us there at top speed!"

"Aye-aye, Captain," grinned Iggy.

But though the super-sub soared through the saltwater at an incredible speed, Don Leo was catching up!

"We *must* keep ahead of him, Iggy!"
urged Teggs.

Cripes pointed to a big block of metal
ahead of them. "There's the floating
factory!"

"Does it have a packing room?" asked
Teggs. "You know, like the one I got
trapped in on the wreck?"

"Sure it does," said Cripes. "Iggy, head
for the intake pipe round the side. It'll
take you straight there. But I still don't
see—"

"No time for explanations now," said
Teggs, as they shot through the pipe and
into the loading area. "I'm getting off!
Park the sub and wait for me."

"But Don Leo's right behind us!"
protested Iggy. "If he sees you, he'll eat
you!"

"I hope he *tries*," smiled Teggs. "My
plan depends on it!"

Iggy parked the super-sub just outside
the packing room. As it bobbed about

on the surface of the water, Teggs jumped out and quickly waded over to another large pipe, half-filled with water. Designed to let through tons of shelled ammonites for packing, it was easily big enough to fit a stegosaurus.

And, with a bit of a squeeze, a livid liopleurodon.

Don Leo suddenly burst out of the water beside Teggs, ready to bite. His terrifying teeth missed Teggs's neck by millimetres.

"Phew!" whistled Teggs. "You know, I think I liked Mira a whole lot better than Don Leo!"

"I'll like you a whole lot better when you're lining my stomach!" growled Don Leo.

"Don't hold your breath," said Teggs. He bashed Don Leo on the nose with his tail.

"Come here!" Don Leo roared in anger.

Teggs waded off down the pipe, with the liopleurodon slithering along right behind him, trying to squeeze through.

A few seconds later, Teggs splashed out into the packing room. Panting for breath, he turned on the machines. The conveyor belt jerked forwards. Metal scoops swung down from the ceiling.

Don Leo wriggled along through the shallow water after Teggs. He looked *furious*.

"Catch me if you can!" cried Teggs.

He climbed up onto the clanking
conveyor belt.

"I'll chase you onto dry land if I have
to!" snarled Don Leo. Somehow he
managed to flip himself out of the
water and onto the conveyor belt
behind Teggs.

Now they were both heading straight
for the wrapping machine.

Don Leo laughed nastily. "I've got
you now, you stupid stegosaur!"

Teggs just smiled. "Actually, I think you'll find that . . . *I've got you!*"

Just before he could fall into the wrapping machine, Teggs jumped off the conveyor belt. He hit the water with an enormous splash. But it was too late for Don Leo. He couldn't flip himself out of the way in time.

"No!" yelled the liopleurodon as he tumbled into the wrapping machine.

Teggs held his breath as the machine rattled and shook. Then it bulged like a balloon. Steam started to spurt from its insides.

Finally, out popped Don Leo, all wrapped up on a long plastic tray. Only his head, tail and flippers were left sticking out.

"Get me out of here!" yelled the liopleurodon, struggling furiously.

But the conveyor belt moved him quickly on. He was tipped into a large wooden crate. Robot arms placed the lid on top and nailed it in place. Finally the crate was shoved off into the water with a big splash.

"There," said Teggs. "That should hold you till you've calmed down a bit!"

"What about my ship?" came Don Leo's muffled voice.

"I think your test flight is over," said Teggs. "That ship will never fly again. But your crew are still safely sleeping. If you promise to be good, I'm sure the cryptoclidus will help you all get back home to your own planet."

"And what if we're *not* good?" said Don Leo.

"I was sent here by the Dinosaur Space Service. They'll be watching you very closely," Teggs said sternly. "If you know what's good for you . . . behave!"

Just then, Iggy and Cripes splashed into the packing room.

"You did it!" beamed Iggy.

"At last, we can get on with our fishing in peace," said Cripes.

"As soon as you've helped Don Leo and his friends get back home," said Teggs. "But don't worry. I think he'll be better behaved from now on!"

"Suppose so," grumbled Don Leo from his crate.

"Well, I think that about *wraps things up* here," chuckled Teggs. He spoke into his communicator. "Arx? Gipsy? It's Teggs. Mission accomplished!"

Gipsy's voice crackled out: "Well done, Captain!"

"Admiral Rosso will be delighted!"
added Arx.

"Get the shuttle ready," Teggs ordered.
"Then let's all grab dinner somewhere
dry." He grinned at Iggy. "I'm ready for
a ten course banquet – with a big, new
adventure for dessert!"

THE END

TALKING DINOSAUR!

TRICERATOPS –
try-SERRA-tops

STEGOSAURUS –
STEG-oh-SORE-us

BAROSAURUS –
bar-oh-SORE-us

IGUANODON –
ig-WA-noh-don

HADROSAUR –
HAD-roh-sore

DIMORPHODON –
die-MORF-oh-don

CRYPTOCLIDUS –
cript-oh-CLIE-dus

LIOPLEURODON –
LIE-oh-PLUR-oh-don

ASTROSAURS
BOOK FOUR

THE MIND-SWAP MENACE

Read the first chapter here!

Chapter One

SPACE WRECK!

The spaceship was in a hurry. Shaped like an enormous metal egg, it shot past stars and planets at top speed.

Its name was the DSS *Sauropod*. It was the fastest ship in the Dinosaur Space Service.

It was on a vital mission.

And it was about to crash at ten million miles per hour into something that shouldn't be there at all . . .

"Red alert!" squawked the alarm pterosaur, the moment she noticed. Her screeching voice echoed throughout the *Sauropod*. "Unknown object ahead! We're going to crash! *Squaaaaaawk!*"

"Hit the brakes!" yelled Captain Teggs

Stegosaur from his control pit. "Fast!"

The *Sauropod* spun and skidded as it started to screech to a halt. Teggs clamped his teeth around a huge clump of ferns and held on for dear life.

"Object straight ahead!" reported Gipsy, clinging to her chair. "Can we steer around it?"

"Not while we're spinning like this," Teggs cried. "Arx, will we stop in time?"

"It's going to be close," Arx said. A dozen dimorphodon grabbed hold of his horns to stop him sliding away from his controls. "Oh, no! The brakes are burning out!"

"Don't worry, they won't let us down," gasped Iggy, hanging onto a safety rail. He knew the ship like the back of his claw. "I built those brakes myself! They can handle worse than this."

"You mean it can *get* worse than this?" gasped Gipsy. Her head crest flushed bright blue with alarm.

At last, with a final flip, the *Sauropod* came to a stop.

"I told you we'd make it," grinned Iggy.

"It was close, though," said Arx, as a dimorphodon wiped sweat from his horn.

"Switch on the scanner!" cried Teggs. "Let's see what's out there!"

More dimorphodon flocked to obey. On the screen, Teggs and his crew could see something that looked like a big, silver wheel, slowly spinning.

"Looks like a space station of some kind," said Arx.

"It's not on any of the space maps," said Gipsy. "I've sent a greetings message but there's no reply."

Teggs pointed at the screen with his spiky tail. "Maybe *that* would explain why!"

A huge, black, jagged hole had been torn in the shell of the space station.

"This is a wheel with a puncture," said Iggy. "Must be a space wreck!"

"It doesn't look very old," said Gipsy. "I wonder where it came from?"

"I don't recognize the design," said Arx. But as the wheel kept turning, he suddenly saw a blood-red sign on the silver surface. It was a dinosaur skull with rows of jagged teeth.

A shiver crept up the long, bony spines of the astrosaurs. They all knew that this design was the mark of meat-eaters . . .

Read the rest of
THE MIND-SWAP MENACE
to find out what lurks on board
the sinister space wreck!

Find your fantastic **ASTROSAURS** collector cards in the back of this book. More cards available in each **ASTROSAURS** title. You can also add to your collection by logging on to

www.astrosaurs.co.uk